D0760248

In the Sweet Balance of the Flesh

Lee Meitzen Grue

Cover art by Moonyeen McNeilage

Library of Congress Number: 90-061587
ISBN: 0-911051-55-4

*

My thanks to the members of The New Orleans Poetry Forum for their
precise and insightful criticism, and to Yusef Komunyakaa and Martha
McFerren for further suggestions on the final manuscript.

Poems in this book originally appeared in **Negative Capability,
Southwest Poetry Journal, Balcones, Louisiana Literature,
The Mississippi Valley Review, Black River Journal,
Women's Art Journal, Trains and Other Intrusions (a
chapbook), Phase and Cycle, Poem, Roberts Writing
Awards, Nexus, The Signal, Fiddlehead, Free Lunch,
Pontchartrain Review, Piedmont Literary Review, Pawn
Review, Texas Review, Ploughshares, Tinderbox,** and
Xavier Review.

Time to write was supported by a grant from The National Endowment
for the Arts. The publication of **In The Sweet Balance of the
Flesh** was supported in part by a grant from the New Orleans Jazz and
Heritage Foundation.

Plain View Press
P.O. Box 33311
Austin, TX 78764

Table of Contents

Artwork by Jim Gabour

Above the River

willows lean and intersect,

not to disturb anything,
things as they are without intrusion,
without a *pardon me* as I stumble
over the feet of the speakers,
I've wanted eyes

like wrap-around windows. Clear-cut panes
to flap
over river, hard city, gulf
waves in tight curls moving toward the marsh,

to find sky fish to school with
not wanting to loop the loop
back
              to the body
with needs
small hungers.

Just windows
like wide goggles on the invisible man,
the Baron's empty helmet,
a scarf
trailing fringes in the air.

Ripe Olives

I have a craving for you
like ripe olives,
a lifting of the hairs
on the nape of my tongue.
My flesh yearns toward you,
I'm sick inside at the flick
of your eye.

A poisonous question coiled in my throat
can't be asked,
all I have is dumb show.
When my emptiness holds your hard flesh

your self eludes my touch,
you wear a thin brittle shell
soft in the cracks of old wounds.
We kiss,
our lips click like the beaks of wild birds,
tongues reach out to touch selves
but sling weakness,
sharp words slice vital parts.

Let's go to bed:
shed your snakeskin, turtle shell, beetle husk,
meet me close and warm,
tomorrow we arm ourselves
and part.

Ed's Skateland: Chalmette

Mr. Willie guards the till,
a cigar stuck in his smile.
One ticket buys privilege,
opening
a door to the Imperial Waltz
where a ball of myriad lights
prisms the floor,
pink blaze, green shadows flying after.
This is the hall where
remembrance is made.
A slender boy holds the waist
of a girl,
his right hand tight at her backbone,
his head cocked.
She is the handle of a dream
through which he spins,
this is the waltz without effort,
the walls blur,
nothing between them
will fly beyond this spiral.
They are the eye around which winds
reel,
if only,
if only,
the music would continue,
the record turning,
the needle locked.

Artwork for *Monument to Porkchop*
by James Sohr

Monument to Pork Chop

I read it in the paper.
"Oliver 'Pork Chop' Anderson died
July 2nd on Lesseps Street in the 9th ward,"
just six blocks down.
The picture, a long-faced nephew
at odds with Pork Chop grinning prime
on a poster he'd signed to pay for his funeral.
Not to be because the Dennis Mortuary on Louisiana Avenue
needed money and there wasn't any. Cold feet

strike no fire. In my mind,
Tom Dent and Danny Barker whisper a bitter chorus,
"Hmm—Plantation Time."
But listen Tom—Danny—no shame in Pork Chop dancing.
He wanted to and people wanted to see him.
Artists often die poor,
richest in the work—applause, laughter
can't be banked.

And the Greeks, say count no man happy until you add his life,
like a fugue all the voices will arrive.
A headliner—even the woman at the dry cleaners knew
he'd passed lacking money and sick. Her face told it:
There's my youth gone, dead of cancer
in a three room apartment.
She said, "If you find out more, let me know,"

speaking of someone esteemed she'd lost track of.
And maybe Pork Chop tapping before we changed the laws
knew:
You can dance out before you can walk out.
That's a property of intelligence,
to know what exists and what should be exited.

The Fire Eater

tilting the bottle up
he drinks kerosene like it was
whiskey
then passes forward and back
with the flame
held
on the torch of his hand,
his head moving
like the head of a cobra, his hand
moving to his mouth
lips touch
and he catches fire

the audience drops back
he moves up
the steps of St. Louis Cathedral
like Jesus
        in a miracle
I walk past in my red jacket
for a long   hot look
wanting to spit hot coals
back at him
as he moans   mama
and his tongue shoots flame
under the white hem of my skirt
a slow curl burns in an updraft

but I pass downwind
the fire
smoothing my skirt   a charred
ring of crisp muslin   a bit of soot
on my left shoe

Booker: Black Night Keeps on Falling

Something Stupid must have been a comment,
sometimes Malagueña,
came out like a Liberace tune.
What James Booker played
was here like my mama when I needed it.

He wasn't a young dead man like Robert Johnson
or somebody I don't get to hear much like Blue Lu Barker.

Downtown he played at Lou and Charlie's
or uptown at the Maple Leaf. I'd go
across town to hear him.
There's something free about driving alone
at night, going into a bar
not to drink much or talk,
but to listen—anonymous
as pain,

a kind of emptiness filled like a belly
with dirty rice. Sometimes,
moving down St. Claude Avenue or St. Charles,
I'd ask myself, *What's on your mind?*
You're not black. You're a well-fed white woman living
in the richest country in the world.

I see too much.

Booker and headache powders
at Jimmy's corner store
work for anybody. Blues
feel and fall
all over you into the gaps.
They don't care who you are
because sorrow's common as dirt,
nothing's certain—people go.

Allan

The bell of a tuba broad and bright
as the face of the man it embraced like a brother, the long tube
reaching around his shoulder
on the front page of The Times-Picayune,
Wednesday, March 11, 1987.
"Preservation Hall Founder Dead at 51."
The day already rainy and cold now
moved of its own weight.

People with furled umbrellas
hurried up the wide porch of Sontheimer's Funeral Home.
The crowd moved in quiet tides, multiple shades of faces,
camelhair coats, ponchos, pin-striped suits, and rubber-legged
men who'd come to second line. Mourners, horns
restrained by strings, a banjo,
each note like a mule-drawn wagon—long-faced, dignified.

His wife,
and two sons wearing yarmulke.
One of the sons I know plays the tuba.
The rabbi spoke of the musician's place among us,
when the words were over people gathered on the street.
The first band struck up a slow march, umbrellas
popped, as hundreds began to slow drag the streets
of the Quarter,
following his car drenched in flowers
to a closed
Preservation Hall,

where his life is:
Kid Sheik, Willie Humphrey, or where
life hangs around: Billy Pierce,
Joe Robichaux, Sweet Emma, George Lewis.
The sweat gathers like dew on the benches,
old men and women play all requests one dollar, "The Saints"
five—"St James Infirmary", "Didn't He Ramble." All those
long, long sad songs and raw, hot songs,

bouncing off tobacco-juice walls, jazz
with us long after it's gone.

Christmas

falls like a sashweight
between Thanksgiving and Mardi Gras.

A cold window clouds the heavy green
draining the elephant ears.
Everything is down on the root—wet,
even the roaches in their dirt cribs are paddling.

A walk past St. Louis No. 2,
where bodies float in sunken tubs,
somebody's Christmas piled on an ash heap:
padded sateen crosses, burnt wires, crown-studded
flower piercers, remains of a pink sash.
Oh, you hangers of stockings, pine cone gatherers,
curlers of ribbons, writers of checks,
Santa Claus sleeps under the green green grass,

and I am girding my loins for happiness,
like the skinny man with a goosepimpled butt in a stall
at the bus station, knowing
it is momentary, spasmodic—hard
to keep up.

Give me the children's list.
What do they need?
I can tell you
you can't get it at Zayre's, K-Mart, or J.C. Penny.
You can't get it for more money at Hausmann's
or at Sak's for plastic.
Every year they praise it on cards,
but nobody's got the price, the ticket,
or even a clue.

This is the wrap-up
in pretty paper: The rain has stopped,
tires lick at the wet pavement,
go up into a dark garage,
where I go down the elevator
to the first floor of D.H. Holmes:
The candy counter is chocolate in gold and red foil,
the perfumes loll around fat-bottled
smoking exotic oils,
behind the counters are women in Monteil masks,
I go up to them to get what I can,
cheap.

Hard Freeze

Off Decatur by the Seven Seas
a bare neck gawks out of a khaki blanket,
swaddled like a wino by the back step
a yard faucet runs at the nose.

Lengths of exposed pipe
snake and stagger aimless,
bent-elbowed
under the slave-quarters next door,

jakelegged—unprotected,

like the stubbled man asleep on cardboard
down the block,
they'll freeze and crack.

January on Julia Street

No drunks out tonight.
Cold warehouses press against the lean street.
Flapping canvas wrinkles around
clouded windows yellow at the edges
like the eyes of old men
watching the past come around again.

Red-eyed in the night
reflectors on parked cars light up.
It's cold out.
White paper sticks like bandages
to streets flowing slick

with the blood of traffic lights.
Our tin shield rolls between sidewalks,
the empty street's an ache sucked in.

They're gone off Julia.
Winter's winos are cold-stored with the rats
in the drafts of high-raftered packing houses.
For warmth and a can of beans
they light a fire and burn us out.

Arnold

the cold

with no fist or rag
stuffed into it
sings off the highway
rushes teeth
tastes gums,
a faint trickle
bleeds in your throat,

the woman clings to your back
like you cling to the bike,

relishes

chicken-fried steak and milk-gravy in truck stops,
peeing in gas station toilets,

guys named Lobo, R. Lee, and Smiley
glad to see you with grunts of "Maybe,"
and a half-cup of coffee,

always a destination:
Thomas & Charley, Matamoros,
a rally in Acapulco,

she's a girl again
because you're seventy-six
but horny

and she's sure you'll
never die but you do

up against a truck.

Marbles

everytime we dig
pocked agates
milky white
cracked blue
as the eye
of a blind man

along the earth
my fingers raise
ancient glass
dim as a fish bowl

in this yard
the earth moves
in measured rolls

I met a man
crooked as a ginger root
who said
he was the boy
who played in this house

if so
there's more concerned here
than time

a fine hand moved
to split them all
for keeps

Traveling Cheap

Gold, gold, and cheap motels, I've got to hand it to us, we didn't do much, but we saw everything. Chili—how many cafes have chili? A hundred, a thousand. Or how about the night in the Navajo motel, one of the better ones—Fair night, everybody crazy-excited—a few rides and something wonderful going to be. A woman jumped out of a red pickup, let it roll away, the Navajo policeman caught it like a wild horse. A shame our timing was off, I read about the parade in the "Navajo Observer." Miss Bequey, the Representative's daughter was Queen, Indian Veterans of Vietnam rode floats, there was a riderless horse. I got chili peppers, corn husks, and a sheep's head at the Navajo supermarket, and when we ordered one piece of fried bread with chili on it at the gas-pump cafe, the Apache with a stringy beard gave us extra food, and said, "Don't tell." He thought we were broke and couldn't afford two. It made us feel good. We thanked him and ate it. Once in Mexico we were broke and the waiter took the refries. And the grand Canyon was suitably grand, and sometimes I'm glad we travel cheap like when I didn't have to go down the trail on a donkey because it cost too much or below the rim in a helicopter because that did too. In Oregon all those people talking about dredging for gold, the guy who told us how old salmon tastes bad, how fish snap at roe on a hook to save it, get caught in the process. I saw them struggle upstream at the Bonneville Dam. In a tin shed workmen slit females, eject eggs and fertilize them in a bucket with milt jacked off the males. Pretty basic. Look at old salmon, you'll know what they mean by long in the tooth. Self-denial and death, that's what reproduction's about. And I'm calling home like a madwoman—"Hey, kids, everything, OK? Sure?" How about the Rogue Elk Hotel where the sign said: **Built in 1914. Slept in by Zane Grey and President Hoover.** Old grey Zane must have snuggled with Hoover, the bed that little. We didn't eat the free breakfast—just coffee. In the cafe *beaucoup* chess players— international chess by satellite. At the counter, eyes the color of Tahoe, the most beautiful man ... Sometimes I felt older because so many people traveling are retired. They smiled like conspirators. Sometimes I felt young, giddy—no children, and doing what we wanted: Taking a logging road that ended at the top of the mountain—throwing rocks out of the road, backing over obsidian like tire-cutters at a parking lot, breath cut off until we found ourselves, the same afternoon, walking hand in hand on a swept beach in California looking for shells where there weren't any just to bring something back, finally settling for the chimney shape of an old barnacle, incredible what it costs us, souvenirs.

Artwork for *Moroccan Henna* by Suzi

Moroccan Henna

orange-red
stains leather, hair, the hoofs and manes
of horses,
        fingernails and feet of Moslem women.

The specialist smokes cigarettes
draws with an empty syringe
dunked in green paste,
on hands,
the gold-lettered box sensuous as a drug stash.

A red hen walks in the yard
stretching her leg,
a *djinn* lives in the drain
angry from scalding water.
Henna placates.

Stains, stains
on the three-year-old
prepared for Ramadan in her best dress,
paraded in the *medina*, hen tracks
on chubby fingers
stiff with paste.

When the blood came no henna,
before the month of Fate and Cloth
for distraction, and after the seventh month
attention to the body weary with child.
Three days of close regard
against tradition: *Do not transform or denature
his work.*

The specialist is paid cash,
has a tray of sweets,
a five-pound can of sugar,
she is a woman of questionable status, smokes,
drinks. Draws for three days to music.

The decorated woman is proud,
the room smells good,
essence of orange blossom, sugar
mixed with paste.
Someday she will go to Fez and Marrakesh
where they are known for intricate design,
get drunk on incense, sips of orange water, dance
spasmodic jerks suggestive to women only, jacknife around
scarves, whipped hair,
fall down in a trance until the *djinn* tire and leave
her body.

Murals in the Minoan Room at the Athens Museum

The young priestess
from the West House with pursed lips, teal hair
offers
and I accept,
as the daughter of a woman
whose breasts fell and black hair
in the same shape as the pictured body
with outstretched arms.

This is the room.
I am the fisherman with skeins
of mustard and turquoise fish, my skin
brown, my hips slim, and oh,
here I am again naked and boxing
with my friend Adolescere, our sway-backed
bellies leaning forward, my beads falling
over my arm as I sock her doe-eye, toe to toe.

And here I sway papyrus, leap monkey to monkey among
the kissing birds in static flight, there the buck
and doe speak in tongues, the thick black
outline of their backs suspend slight hooves
above nothing, here
my simple boat glides, we all sit stiffly as the dolphins
fly over us, below us, I am sky
as the plaster flakes and the sun fades.

Torogo Gorge: Taiwan

A mountain
wind
on the edge,
leaps
like a suicide.

Pieces of torn paper
fly upward into my hand.

At the lodge
my mind leaves the flat garden's
red poinsettias,
walks out to yellow butterflies

to
hang still

fall
against rock,
drown in the surge
sluiced away like silt.

The sun surfaces, moves up

one knob of rock

then darkness palpable.

I catch my breath by the screen door
as twelve red lanterns
light the corners of the high pagoda.

The Rabbit Lesson: Vietnam

Where is the rut in the road, bumps
along mud fields that stretch forever?
Graceful birds fly,
there's noise, a plume of smoke,
the jeep low gears past butchers' bones
and parts of old dolls,
smiling at this fantasy we jump down
to dance and whoop our joy
while we count:

Sometimes we count the pieces,
sometimes those who walked,
we cheat a little to up our score,
and every piece I count is not me,
and is not meaning.
Sunday school boys tack good marks
on bulletin boards,
zeroes and ones, ones and zeroes,
real numbers.

Survivors walk the streets,
awesome and ordinary.

Fields

Crows running like dogs across an open corn field,

the train from Bratislava to Budapest
gathers like a combine, land
familiar as Texas is tucked under.
I never leave home.
It races after me like my shadow
sewn to my feet by coarse black thread.

Back there on the bay hill, Uncle Buttons stands
handing me his shotgun. It's greasy,
This shot some black birds—fifty cents apiece.
Give it to your boys.

Arrogant with mother love I hand it back.
My sons don't hunt.
That was before one bought a shotgun,
the other registered.

Eight thousand miles away,
I'm traveling over fields where farmers harvest
shrapnel, the crows heavy with corn
scramble up the slope like men loaded with ammunition.

Nametag

Sun... too much sun.
The sea flaps white sheets on a distant line.
Norfolk pines... black cut-outs on a blue sky.
His hair draws me like fire.
Thin, blistery skin—pink.
Greenish sunglasses loom
as he smiles into my face.
This name: *Gunning*
              Port Brazos, Texas
Big enough to read.

At a picnic
in Queenscliff, Australia
we talk of names, history, the Irish.
His father's family—immigrants to the U.S.
Twelve children at Ellis Island waiting
for parents gone to town
and killed
in a streetcar accident.
The kids adopted out—lost.
The name: *Gunning*.
He looks for it.
Sometimes one
in a phone book in a distant city.

I would like to see his eyes.

The wife comes up—talks.
Five bedrooms, three kids,
Port Brazos, Texas.

Death of the Rainmaker among the Dinka

1

A voice in the ground,
people shuffle their feet,
a cough from a man
leaning on a stick.
The voice rose
and wavered
like heat above dust.

Rain
god of our people
dust or flood
my tongue
passed the word.

Children stared at the sun,
spots danced
as vision
passed from them,
they could not see the man
in the grave
of his own choosing.

The cold voice said much
the dusty old   nodded.
Rounded words
heavy on his chest,
will lifted to the edge.

2

The rainmaker dying
words falling on the sand.
Young men shifted their sex
with light gestures
and smiled whitely,

seeing the heat
in the young men's eyes
the virgins scooped sand
under their aprons.

Children bellied up
to warm legs,
the legs walked away.
Dusty men
waited for the sun to fall.

3

One stayed
listening
to distant thunder,
a history of the tribe.

The boy smelled rain,
willed rain,
rain fell.

Old men at the edge,
pushed red mud onto the rainmaker's face,
he passed from life.

Hump-backed
old digging sticks
walked home.

The boy felt red dust
in his throat,
weight on his chest.

Artwork for *Daisy the Singing Chimp Moves to the Bush*
by James Sohr

Daisy the Signing Chimp Moves to the Bush

Your fingers spoke

of simple things
deliberate,
as the pronouncements of Buddhist monks,
but nothing of the animal we hadn't heard before.

In Norman, Oklahoma, your human parents grow older,
there's the weariness of middle age.
Death is coming and Papa wants a sports car.
The great talking-monkey dream is packed up
with love beads and tie-dye,
and you're not a cute little jocko anymore,

so now
a plane has dropped you in Gambia
with other displaced chimps, except for
Toots and Joe who went on to labs,
and a woman who tries hard to be a monkey.

You pick at a few Netto seed pods
conveniently dumped, feeling
a bit run down from hookworm picked up on the trail,
you wonder about the folks in Norman,
the old man like a tired orangutan drooped
before the T.V. listening
to the President rattle his sci-fi,
and when the monkey in the moon lights up
the fever trees
you just want somebody to talk to.

The Biographer

You are so much more interesting than I.
Your mother was lost, mad, and beautiful.
Understandable were the blue rages which consumed
your father the doctor.

Unmistakable the charm of your lover,
who threw his brace on the bedroom floor,
took off his leg and hopped to the bathroom.

Your book bound in red leather, the collected works,
is small but exquisite:
Its binding exudes richness like a perfect sauce.
See, reading it for the twentieth time
I've notched the ribbon—threads unravel—checked
the lining of your purse, used your lipstick,
lost your gloves.
Taking a cat, I call her St. Agnes,
and feed her, as you did, sweetbreads only.

Tomorrow I'm interviewing your husband.
He's bringing your black fur,
I'll put it on after dinner.
He'll escort me home in the snow
                    by cab,
come up for a drink, touch my hair,
follow me
into your bedroom where we'll take up your life.

Your Moroccan friend sent a *gris-gris* packet,
I opened it, took out nail parings,
a drop of blood, pubic hairs,
under the microscope I found them to be organic:
You lived.

This is the mystery. All of it,
a life that is. Under
the microscope—open—hidden.
There's time to taste it,
to savor sweet *majoun*,
the aftertaste
a bitter capsule.

A Few Words from Gretel after the War

Hansel, I believe we have caused
great mischief.
Mothers told our story
to German children
who wove it into their dreams.

They knew we were children also.
That we too followed bread
back to our beginnings.
That our parents could not feed us
and twice left us in the woods alone.

They thought
we should have the sugar house,
stuff out stomachs
with the whole frame,
yea,
with the whole country,

and they knew you were trapped, Hansel,
put in a cage:
They saw your finger
as a real bone,

and when we pushed her
into the oven
they rejoiced.

Later,
when oily smoke
stood over Germany,
they said:
Don't worry.
It's only our witches burning.

Nijinsky: The Paris Tour

*All I gain in profit is my keep in the best hotels
and a seat at the Russian Ballet.*
                                        Diaghilev

Company couldn't open him, so
they thought him a little stupid.
For performances he bought hundreds of
dancing shoes from London, of a special kid,
and for rehearsals wore pastel shirts,
crepe de chine luxuriously thin,
then walked through his part mechanically,
the dancers whispering,
"Nijinsky doesn't understand his role."

But make-up changed him. His mauve skin
shimmered, his body, the silver blade
of a golden knife, among pearls, amid silk,
feathers of peacock, firebird; a slave
in a harem clothed by Bakst and Stravinsky's
cascades of arpeggio exasperating the orchestra,
                the season turning
                        to the mud grunts of spring.
His body shuddering, gaping for something to emerge,
skin, muscles; eyes
                transformed him to suffering,
and Petrushka,
a grotesque creature
                hanging ungainly in space.
Sarah Bernhardt witnessing said,
"I am afraid,"

and then a costume, a role,
rose petals covering him, suggesting a strange
beetle with a rose petal mouth.
Like the sickness of the rose releases
attar of roses, he, lifting
contrary to laws of flight following so high,
so curved a trajectory, that Jean Cocteau could never
smell a rose without remembering
his phantom leap.

    Le Spectre soared, flew
malgre le nuit qui tombe, paused then fell
      perpendicular,
caught in a net of hands. His masseur and Vassily
massaged his human heart while he shivered
like a lathered Arab, his nostrils opening
      his rose petals dark with sweat.
Mysteriously, after the performance, his costume
fell apart as Vassily sold his petals one by one.
"What do we pay for these moments,"
said the man transformed,
"Closest to God and beast is the miraculous."
The faun, on the floor of the stage,
writhing upon the nymph's veil:
      "un faux pas," dit Paris.

Nijinsky choreographed frenetic
jerks, twists, asymmetrical to new sound in *extremis,*
registers of strings, woodwinds,

and when this animal in rut, the Russian Spring,
exploded on stage,
a maiden danced to death while the people
beat each other on the head
and Ravel, red and raging, cursed them, the audience
booing, hissing like geese, others
as if their seats were on fire, shouted *"Bis, Bis."*

This leap,
this life at twenty-nine,
        a pause
in the air,
     then a fall to a blank stage,
a dance on imaginary glass. Petrushka thrown
by his master
        into the corner of a black box.

Romola Pulszky: Who Became His Wife

Thank you, my Lord. You have permitted me
to live in this century, to see Nijinsky dance.

Romola Nijinsky

1

My desire seized me at the Russian Ballet,
purples, oranges—green: barbaric, Byzantine,
shook me when he took the stage.

My mother was the foremost actress of Hungary:
it was not difficult to carry out my plan;
by guile, by flattery, I used them all:
Bolm, Cechetti, Diaghilev.
I joined Cechetti's class,
not for love of the dance but the dancer.

A late supper at the Savoy,
Nijinsky, Diaghilev, their friends—
Nijinsky, a prince, distant, observing,
eyes half-closed, oblique,
eyes which I adored above all else.
I was there, here, everywhere he appeared
in public.

On tour to Argentina, we left
Diaghilev marooned in Paris by words:
Death by water.

2

At Cherbourg, Le Petit came up the gangplank.
He took off his hat, smiled.
I said to Anna, my maid,
"Here is my chance. No Diaghilev.
What the woman wants, God wants."
Anna arranged my cabin: roses in silver vases,
sepia photos, silk covers, and near my bed,
the miraculous Little Jesus of Prague.
In the ship's salon Baton played Bach,
Nijinsky sunk in the notes danced with his fingers.
To me Baton said, "Go."
Every evening without a word Anna
tore a day off the calendar—smiled.
I was annoyed but said nothing.

Mornings on deck, he practiced;
Mr. Williams, his masseur, waited
holding a silk, green dressing gown.
From Williams I learned
the whole of him, each muscle separately, his sinews—
the iron bolt of his thighs.
After weeks, I cried:

"I'm sick of it!"

But something pulled me:
Nijinsky half-leaning against the rail, in **Smoking,**
holding a small black fan ornamented

with one gold rose. Rapidly fanning himself,
his eyes half-closed, so slanted. He
slightly inclined his head, an imperceptible nuance.
I said,

"Vaslav Fomitch, you have forgotten—I have
the little pillow your mother sent you."
In Russian, "Keep it."
I could have choked him—one day more to Rio.

Absorbed in his art,
it is true he had no interest in women,
but sometimes didn't I catch a smile.

3

We were sitting in the bar before lunch.
Dimitri said,
"Romola Carlovna, Nijinsky can not speak himself;
he has requested me to ask you in marriage."
It was no joke though I locked myself away crying, a note
under my door said, "Nijinsky is waiting."
On deck Nijinsky said, *"Mademoiselle, voulez vous?
Vous et moi"*, *a*nd pantomimed a ring
on the left hand.
Ah, my miraculous Little Jesus of Prague.

No one believed it. They said he was heartless.
The friendship with Diaghilev—more.
I listened to nothing.
Better to be unhappy serving genius
than to live without it.

"Anna," I said, "The cart has given me a lift."

Anna was there, in Buenos Aires,
when the priest asked in Spanish,
"Will you always stay by him
in happiness as well as misfortune,
in health and sickness forever""
I promised and he blessed us.
We should have lived happily ever after, but
there was Diaghilev, and God, and war . . .

Nijinsky, His Final Performance: January, 1919

We are an infinite part of God in the universe,
when we create something beautiful, we reflect Him.
                                    Nijinsky

It was in a straight-backed chair
carried out onto the stage
he sat, staring motionless
at the well-bred
for half-an-hour or so.
Uneasily, they shifted in their seats.
The furs of the women went slinking
up the aisles trying to get out.
Rustling their programs, men moved
their eyes to the floor, to the ceiling,
to exit doors where invisible boxcars called
for the children.
Bolts of black velvet, white velvet, rolled
from the wings. Nijinsky stooped
to form a lush cruciate on the scuffed floor.
He stood then with an open gesture of both arms:
"Now I will dance you the War."

And he lifted his body from the stage,
floating over the bodies of the dead.
The people, breathless, springing
with him, faced horror,
his strength carried them above it, his light being
flying over, as if grace could escape,
    but even the Crucifer could not remain aloft, he
fell, at last,
        the audience with him, crumpled
in the hope of his dream, gasping, choked on his art,

as on a winter morning the world outside, inhaled
the thin crisp air yellow with mustard gas.

My Hair

       like a rope
into night
where unbound it falls from my shoulders
a cloak,
and in it I ride a horse called Frenzy.

I can go anywhere in my long, white nightgown
and my long, red hair.
Oh, these are strange things we're speaking of,
strength in numbers and a power over love,
but when I come upon despair,
I cut my hair.

What is dead within me
falls upon the floor
like dry red leaves fall
I am what I was no more.
But it grows even on a corpse,

and on the woman merely testing
it grows back on her head
like green grass on fresh dirt,
something living on the dead,
something dead on the living: hair.

Living on the strength of it:
I bind wounds, make potions,
pledge for favors, spin it into gold,
pull my love in the window, let the witch out.
I wash the feet of god.

But all this power makes me sick.
I bind it up, stab it with wire sticks.
A woman with tranquil snakes
coiled around her face.

Stacking Them Up

I'm less than I was.
When I sleep I see ulnas,
opalescent-green but friendly,
long and elegant, these are bones
I recognize: They are my mother's
on a stone couch, posed
in her easy living slouch.

I'm too conversant
I know now
what to say to the bereaved.
I can order flowers by the price,
sit up at the wake, eat chicken thighs
and dirty rice at coffin-side.

I used to get mad and fight.
My mother and I fought cancer
with bar bells, sand bags,
and a physiotherapist.
I laid on hands and we visualized.
We never gave up.

"Hey," I used to say, while staggering around
looking for my sweet doctor,
"Things should feel good or hurt."
And I bandaged all my buddies at the bar,
I hurt for everybody.

In the family plot
there are arguments about who goes where:
Who goes in the ground, who goes on top;
nobody knows the order, and that's what
we've been made to believe in, order.
And the order is: Everybody goes.

It's the repetition pulling me down.

Bread

1

My friend bought a loaf of white bread
for sandwiches,

she said:—"Hand me the mayonnaise.
Something's wrong, I can't find my life.
It's fat. My husband drinks beer.
See this—my good bones are covered with

bread.
   Everything goes well.
Each week we buy a toy:
Apple, Cuisinart.
Play with it on Saturday.

Yesterday, my husband sat on the edge
of the tub, fingered
my hair.
Said, 'You're pretty.'
I offered him everything:
physical,
spiritual.
He said, 'Well, I don't know...'

2

My father gave me his death,
I'm his only child—daughter and son.
My mother said, 'Do something. I can't sleep for
gold.'
I carried Krugerands,
to the safety deposit, met

my first lover revolving
in the bank door,
'Here I am again,' he whistled.
'I've got you, dear.'

I said, 'Remember my father?'

'Sure, I stole his car.'

He's dead.

'What do you know!'
We've all got to go
sometime.
'Smell my neck, honey—just been to the hairdresser,
blow-dried—powdered and shaved.
I'm your cocaine.'

I buried him.

Now my mother calls—says,
'My own rare bird, don't go too far,
it's dangerous.'

What I want to know is
where? How far? Just a little—
I want it, so I'll know
who's dead."

Stout Grove: California Redwoods

When the myth was made
the car was a Model-T
straddled by living wood,
brief men wore big moustaches
on a rust-dappled postcard.

This tree is
fallen like a giant
in a suit of bright green moss.

Lie back
dream upward
toward a sky of shivered silk umbrellas,
smell wood going back to earth,
as the dead self is laid out
in a glade like a princess,

and you, off in your own vision
of a wood, call rather than kiss me awake
to see, where fire has eaten out the core
consumed and rising up its own chimney,

what a living thing can live without,
and what force life has
charging up the thin cells
scarcely thicker than skin.

Quarantine in Room 202 at the Corinth Hotel in Mississippi

Pulled to the sills
feverish windowshades block the sun.
A fan turns away from the bed, where I'm basting
in Chicken-Little flannel pajamas.
Weak-eyed, my sight gathers, knots
at the flashlight my mother holds
on Sheena, Queen of the Jungle. She reads aloud,
an endless stack of comic books without covers
donated to the measley one by the druggist.
We are trapped in Submarine 202, dead
on the bottom. The paddle of a key with that number
lies on the bedside table, mordant, moribund,
like a tongue cut out.
The floor above swims with reef life,below:
The desk bell pings, a piano rolls,
"Chatanooga Choo Choo" and fried chicken smells
drift upward.
The food sounds begin, end
in two hour clusters.
A knock at the door—a tray appears,
the pariahs feed on cream of wheat, dry toast.
Nightfall cuts sound off around us
like a silent propeller. Only my mother's hoarse voice
flies solo at midnight. Each word springs
as Sheena leaps vines in the jungle. I grow stronger
on toast, Sheena—the red peppery measles,
feverless I'm reborn
a gingham phoenix,
and my mother, the real winner,
two weeks hanging from her chest like dry teats,
hitches her fourteen empty days,
slings them like a bandolier,
and swaggers down to the bar for a drink.

Sunspots

The sun unlike the earth
and other rigid bodies

is energy transported
outward to the visible,

blotched and spotted,
hottest at the core.
A solar wind blows toward us
particles, imperfect fire,

although changes there
light our midnight skies,
affect magnetic fields

sometimes alter our communications,

once caused the little Ice Age
and the Norse colony to perish.

Daddy, your white anger,
who knows
what generations suffer.

Nyoka the Jungle Girl

Don't be put off by spectator pumps,
neat bun, legs crossed
at ankles. Inside
swing on vines, speak in tongues.

Nyoka
secret name in box. Many people
call other name. *Help! Help!*
Call many people. Say, *Send money.*
Sent Money? Send more money.

Nyoka no let butchers
devastate rain forests,
(Nyoka always refer to self in third person.)
Nyoka merciless to housing developers, slash and burn
agriculturists..

See Nyoka at dentist's office reading New Yorker,
any minute now throw off bra and panties,
swing out on magnolia limb.
Animal self coiled like snake to strike
for: Sierra Club, Anti-Defamation League, Amnesty
International, Civil Liberties, Maryknoll Fathers
(in English and Spanish),
Save the Children, Overture to the Cultural Season,
crack lady who twice in one month collects
to bury dead baby,
St. Cecelia kids selling chances
on a nine passenger van.
Nyoka about to split a seam, run her hose.
Soon Nyoka stand on roof top naked
crying:
Take it! Take it all!

Shell Road

What leaves us
lingers around the track
before it vanishes in dust.

What do I really long for?
Only the flat, shell road,
the dusty grass,
as if what vanished still travels,
and I can't see far enough,
showing up again on the edge
at the same road
while parents ride off in a Packard
to buy soap from the store in town

with only the promise
they'll come back to bathe me.

Grandmother Summers

Tall as Moses treading the wilderness
my grandmother walked out into water,
she leaned on a staff of white wood
and held my hand.
I waded in the beneficence of her straw hat,
a halo of shadow around us,
while the folds of her skirt swirled her legs,
and rough tongues lapped at her hem
like cats licking cream.
My thighs pulled against current, like horses
against harnesses.
Tired by noon
I ate hunks of her homemade bread with sausages,
then dozed afternoon away
on striped ticking puffed as the breast
of the bird with goose down, dreaming of blue
crabs walking string out into water,
summer passing on my grandmother's face
soft as the silver Indian on a nickel.
I woke to the hoarse treadle of her sewing machine
galloping across the back porch,
the canary
thrilled by the gallop, singing his heart out.
I expected to find him, feet in the air
dead from pleasure,
but he was in his cage bathing in a little porcelain tub.
The outside dog moaned
against the screen door, red hens
sang under the dark eaves
of the cistern. I smelled geraniums,
the smell of all red forever,
skinny knees hugged to my chest, senses drunk,
my grandmother's foot on the iron treadle
stitching in black the endless sun
to the white pine floor boards.

Artwork for *Some People Keep Their Houses Up*
by James Sohr

Some People Keep Their Houses Up

Grandfather collected pool tables
like sculpture
or massive skeletons,
a part of the landscape,
age had flayed their green skins
down to slate.
Those tables had played themselves out
onto the porch.
I was a native who never questioned
the greener age before me.

Grandfather was a carpenter,
built solid houses,
but had some superior view of the world.
Some said it was alcohol,
though he quit that.
He never fixed anything—cars,
there were a slew of those flaking
into a pile,
fortresses for red ants.
Dirt daubers plastered under the hoods,
field mice vibrated the upholstery.
I drove those cars to massacres
and poisoned waterholes in Oklahoma.

His land
swallowed machines,
vines grew out of them,
two rent houses burst
from the sticks of lumber he piled in.
His own house teetered on the bay hill,
gray and ready to test the water.
In his world there was no celebration
of the material,
no slapped on paint,
no pilings shoring up the hill,

only the eye of the creator
letting it rot,
walking past it,
smoking his big cigar.

Signed Poem: For the Women Poets

They say old men write best about love.
What then of old women?
Do they moan into the wind?
Do their words curl up like red and gold

paper Chinese prayers stillborn
into air? I know those ancient women
sang of loss. Anonymous,
a hand speckled as a bird's egg
rocked the cradle,

Lully, lullay, lully, lullay
the falcon hath borne my mate away.

And some of them sang the blues knowing
where blues come from,
where blood is common and mysterious
as the moon.

My mother is a stitcher,
she sews them new blue jeans.
My sweetheart is a drunkard, Lord,
down in New Orleans.

Listen, those poets
made poems like quilts, like curtains,
like Irish lace.
They stitched aprons for babies,
sweaters for sons.

Read anonymous as Mary, Martha or Grace
as Faith, Hope or Charity, but also
as a plain woman called Prudence,
who knew her place, kept her distance,
leaving her words as her other works,
unsigned.

Deadly Little Towns

for Janis Joplin and Martha

Driving in
the empty road sucks
at your stomach like a long tube
stuck to your belly button. You left,
but it's got a terrific suction.
You've been meeting lots of people from
here.

Everything's closed. One dog
downtown. Frame buildings hunch
over main street. Thin, passionate,
their backs vacuum-cupped like
consumptive women.
A couple of empty cars pass.

The drugstore's tighter than a drum.
You have to drive twenty-eight miles
to get an ice cream cone. At the gas station
running a comb through his gray hair,
your boyfriend from the fourth grade says,
"You haven't changed."
Janis hadn't
changed. Port Arthur is one, you know.
Gladewater, maybe.

You drive through. Churches. Big, flat school.
The main drag doesn't go anywhere you ever heard of.
Somebody has mown all the yards yesterday.
A big sign says: *A Great Place For Kids.*
Heard of the Big Apple?
This is Orange spitting white seeds everywhere.
That girl with the blonde perm, flat
voice said, "Yeah, everybody's leaving."

The first curve's a doozey. Some people
don't make it. Try the airport. Look
at the windsock. A soft-on.
The planes are in Quonset hangars,
allergic, asthmatic. They've got worms.
Something about this place
makes your gums recede. It's long in the tooth
and Christian—the insurance man wants to save you.

Why did you come back? Because
you've got to see them and they won't leave.
Because they can't—their jobs,
the dogs—the house. Because
the cord doesn't stretch
that far. Because
love breathes out and in.

Valentine

A man stands
in the shower ruminating
like a dumb animal
in the rain, and something awful
on the edge of thought
lurches out of the gray hair on his chest,
slides down the face of his body
to clog up the drain
like the label off a bottle of shampoo.

Has the old pumperoo that puffed up the stairs
ceased wheezing? No, it wants
to say: my heart is heavy,
> my heart aches,
> wants to be a cinnamon red-hot, sticky and sweet,
> to be red-slick paper in a neat envelope,

but no seat of feeling anymore.
He thinks:
> *Better to hold on to this hollow*
> *which roars at night*
> *like the sea in a vacant shell*
> *than replace the pump*
> *with something small, artificial, beastly, or worse*
> *something human.*

Dog Days

In this August heat
no wind reaches the hairless dogs
curled up heavy inside my eyes.
Empty streets
heaved up their wasted bodies,
following
my tongue home
to rest here. They sniff at lies,
their cold noses point failure.
Dead,
they slink
through the dust
looking for you who are not home
in any of the houses.
Waiting for your love or your pity to bury them,
they've taken refuge in my body.
They knock over garbage cans,
forage in my belly,
ache and ache,
whimper around the fence all night.
They will not lie down.
No killing off dead dogs.
Their bones visible,
bellies empty, teeth
as sharp as ever,
they eat from the inside out.

Easter

My house full of chrysanthemums
trying to continue. They stand in dry dirt,
expecting something of me, sun or shade,
I don't know which. If I knew enough about life
to find a good place for them
they'd come back again.
How brave.
The refrigerator's full of eggs, slick
and mottled. Mute as violets.
A birthday, Good Friday, Easter and another
birthday. Days follow each other as they should,

and letters I never write
follow each other
in my head. Dear Fred, Dear Alice, Dear David,
dear, dear me.
My mother once wrote:
If my right arm should happen to fall off
I'd never hear from you again. She's right.
It has. Gallows humor they call it.
A quick grin stretched over the bones.
There's evidence
of winter here in spring.
This morning the knees of my children
cracked like kindling, but overnight
the cat had three kittens. A good sign.

Where did all these messages come from?
A letter like a ship.
Where is it from?
More and more questions and I less quick to answer.
Today I took to water. Let it wash me away.
When the tide came in I heard Babe Stovall play:
Let the circle be unbroken in the sky, Lord, by and by,
holding his steel guitar behind his blue cap,
he played it in my head
surely someone so shiny is still here.

Marilyn

Each hip
like a glass of whiskey
knocked back
swathes the throat
in nude silk
spangled like ice.
Is there anything more real,
more now,
than flesh

promising
to take you out
at least for a minute.
Proud as a rich girl
her fanny says:
Look at me   look at me
each step. . .
You could lose yourself here.
Have you read Proust?

Auras Around Dead Stars

They appear in black and white,
back-splashes of platinum nitrate
around their bodies
quivers like desire.
When they talk—yes, talk,

their voices are hollow but strong
as Hamlet's father.
A drift and run of tides
pull us,
a woman kissing thinks:

The noses—what to do with the noses?
Not remembering the book,
but Bergman's face
come down on by a man
whose lips move past questions.

After they've lost light
we keep the picture:
Bogart's hand around a drink at Rick's,
two fingers with a constant cigarette,
as Sam plays it in the background.

Garbo, a figurehead at the prow,
eyes on the unknown.
In *The Letter* Bette Davis
with outthrust big-eyed breasts,
armed, pumping shots
like sex into a man's body.

A dead star implodes
inside you,
all you can see now, all we can feel now,
as the reel pulls back the non-specific dark,
is total,
         radiance
               escaping

Little Footlet

Good, it's mine and it shall be called
Little Footlet, son of the artist.
                    George Dureau

In the sweet balance of the flesh
lives a son of the artist, studious of pleasure,
elegant as bone,
awakening as a sour taste in a sweet mouth

he demands,
but silently
          jumps around one-legged,
wrestles love, elbows pain,
stumps upstairs,
slides down the bannister,
and jumps a horse:
big ribbed, bony, flatulent.
He is a conquistador,
who rides like thunder into the morning
on unspeakable things said in the night.

Such a small secret hidden away
marches out into the kitchen
makes French toast, hamburgers,
neckbones and greens, settles in to watch T.V.,
eats too much, drinks beer, becomes
a difficult guest, stays longer than
three days, begins to stink like fish.

O Little Footlet, what some people do
in the name of love.

Hey, Jimmy

1

They've gentrified your aunt's house:
Rot is better,
you know I speak of
our own bodies resting under grass.

I want to pull you to me, whisper
like Marlene Dietrich in a bad movie,
Write me—poems.
Writing letters is like coloring in the lines.

So you think you're
in Czechoslovakia followed
by the secret police
just because a mad poet from Florida
records your every word, pretending
it's your life.

I, too, am back in the Gulag,
trying to get my mind situated.
You wrote, *Going to Spain this summer.*
Spain is a whole country like New Orleans.

Even in Spain you pay rent.
It was dry here. Hot
Now rain, weed—red geraniums.

2

At the short end of the morning at Coop's Place
we heard flutes, drums, and a vocal.
Husky, smoky...like mescal.
All those lost nights romanticized
at the shallow end
have caught up
with us swimming for dear life.

It's deeper now, like her voice
on "Body and Soul,"
but we're shrill
TESTING the mike.

                Tell me.
                What is it like?
                What do they do there?

So what
the Rumanian
and the new Beat—*were doing it doggie style.*
Even doggies are silly
doing it.
When you talk about freedom, smile.

Between me and you,
there's hardly enough flag
to lift a wrist.
We're grinding ourselves out.
Better to burn up like roaches.

Hell, I don't mean that,
I'm still clutching my feathered hope.

When we saw the guy in North Beach
scoping the gutter rush, you said,
Some of us didn't make it
through the sixties.

Like poor old Ben
toasting his diabetes with Red Label.
He was so fine I cut off his tie,
and flushed it down the sewers of New Orleans
at an opening for Dureau.
We're still at it,
wading in.
I love the tone of ennui,
such a French movie, but that's not me.
I want my Irish risk.

Meditating wars off like warts
mildews the mind.

I'm glad you were here, old sufi dancer,
shoes into holes,
shoes into holes.
When you get to Majorca
break me off a diamond leaf.

Sewing

      the bobbin reels
my head given over to thread
whirling
off a spool

skin tight
strung out gut thin
trying to sew up
holes

sound as a roach
eating glue off books
in a house full of glass monkeys
not able to mend anything.

Children's Poetry

I entered a conspiracy once
with children, poems
they wrote and I collected
in a book.

Each child wrote something huge
we entered, danced
around in. But some
went deep.

Eric wrote:
underwater
we saw fish
and a great big octopus.
I got caught in the legs of it.
In the Pearl River,
he drowned with his cousin Sonia. She
wrote poems too.

In a dream
after death she told her mother
she likes it at my house.
Lives here now.

Ingrid wrote **The Rainy Day**
taking us into her lonely confidence.
Soon after, a neighbor invited her in,
put her in a box, threw her away
like garbage. Her mother
kept the poetry book
because I need it myself.

Such a deep shaft,
a child's mind
with its dank and branching caverns.
A seam, black and shiny as coal
runs through. Something brought up
burns,
all we see is smoke.
I don't know if we can
bear the light.

Artwork for *The girl Who Could See Through Her Ear*
by Lois Simbach

The Girl Who Could See Through Her Ear

Don't laugh. It's true.
She could see through her ear,
smell through her chin,
a fine gift, and what's more,
things that smelled good to others:
roses, apples, marijuana, fried sausages,
were vile to this girl.

Take them away, she cried.
Give me filth.
And she smelled filth
with great pleasure,
and had to be persuaded
not to dab pig's urine
behind her ears
where she could see it.

And she saw things differently
than others.
She would scope a man
with her left ear,
if he proved handsome,
declare, *Oh, horrors.*
A man covered with squamous warts
presented himself: *My Prince,* she said,
My one, my only true love. He

leaped with delight.
The pair were a great curiosity.
She, with her gift for prediction,
could find rings, hidden money,
and once moved furniture out of the house
before a fire.

He had a gift for adoration,
plied her with lemons and salt.
Delivered green persimmons
for her birthday,
and patiently held books to her ear.
They were happy on the way
to everafter,
when
    the source of her vision changed
to eyes in her stomach, smell
in her heel.
A book placed on her midriff
was read past midnight. She had less use
for the lover,
became concerned with her health.
Counting worms in her intestines,
precisely thirty-three, she
treasured them.
Threw herself into the pleasures
of a dissolute life.
You've changed, he said.
Is love over?

She said, *It is confining and smells bad.*
It is not so ugly or long as art.
Besides, who are you, and why do you ask?

Halloween

The night's
empty hootings,
the stair long and dark,
I must keep my cat in.

Hate
like the black vein in a shrimp
rises headless from us
on well primed occasions.
This night confides how children
love noise.

Radiations of interior discord
masquerade in uniform
saying it is not I.

Old forces in new forms,
the sorcerer's apprentice still unwise.

In the Sweet Balance of the Flesh is printed in a limited first edition of 1000 copies the first 400 of which are signed and numbered.